For little weather adventurers everywhere	For my little Tom, who loves BIG puddles
– S.G.	– D.S.

With special thanks to Dr Lucinda Spokes
for her contribution and advice.

First published 2025 by Nosy Crow Ltd
Wheat Wharf, 27a Shad Thames
London, SE1 2XZ, UK

Nosy Crow Eireann Ltd
44 Orchard Grove, Kenmare,
Co Kerry, V93 FY22, Ireland

www.nosycrow.com

ISBN 978 1 80513 324 7 (HB)
ISBN 978 1 80513 325 4 (PB)

Nosy Crow and associated logos are trademarks
and/or registered trademarks of Nosy Crow Ltd.

Published in collaboration with the University of Cambridge.

Text © Saskia Gwinn 2025
Illustrations © Daniela Sosa 2025

The right of Saskia Gwinn to be identified as the author and Daniela Sosa
to be identified as the illustrator of this work has been asserted.

All rights reserved.

This book is sold subject to the condition that it shall not,
by way of trade or otherwise, be lent, hired out or otherwise circulated in
any form of binding or cover other than that in which it is published.
No part of this publication may be reproduced, stored in a retrieval system,
or transmitted in any form or by any means
(electronic, mechanical, photocopying, recording or otherwise)
without the prior written permission of Nosy Crow Ltd.

The publisher and copyright holders prohibit the use of
either text or illustrations to develop any generative machine learning
artificial intelligence (AI) models or related technologies.

A CIP catalogue record for this book is available from the British Library.

Printed in China following rigorous ethical sourcing standards.

1 3 5 7 9 8 6 4 2 (HB)
1 3 5 7 9 8 6 4 2 (PB)

teeny tiny science

I see a cloud

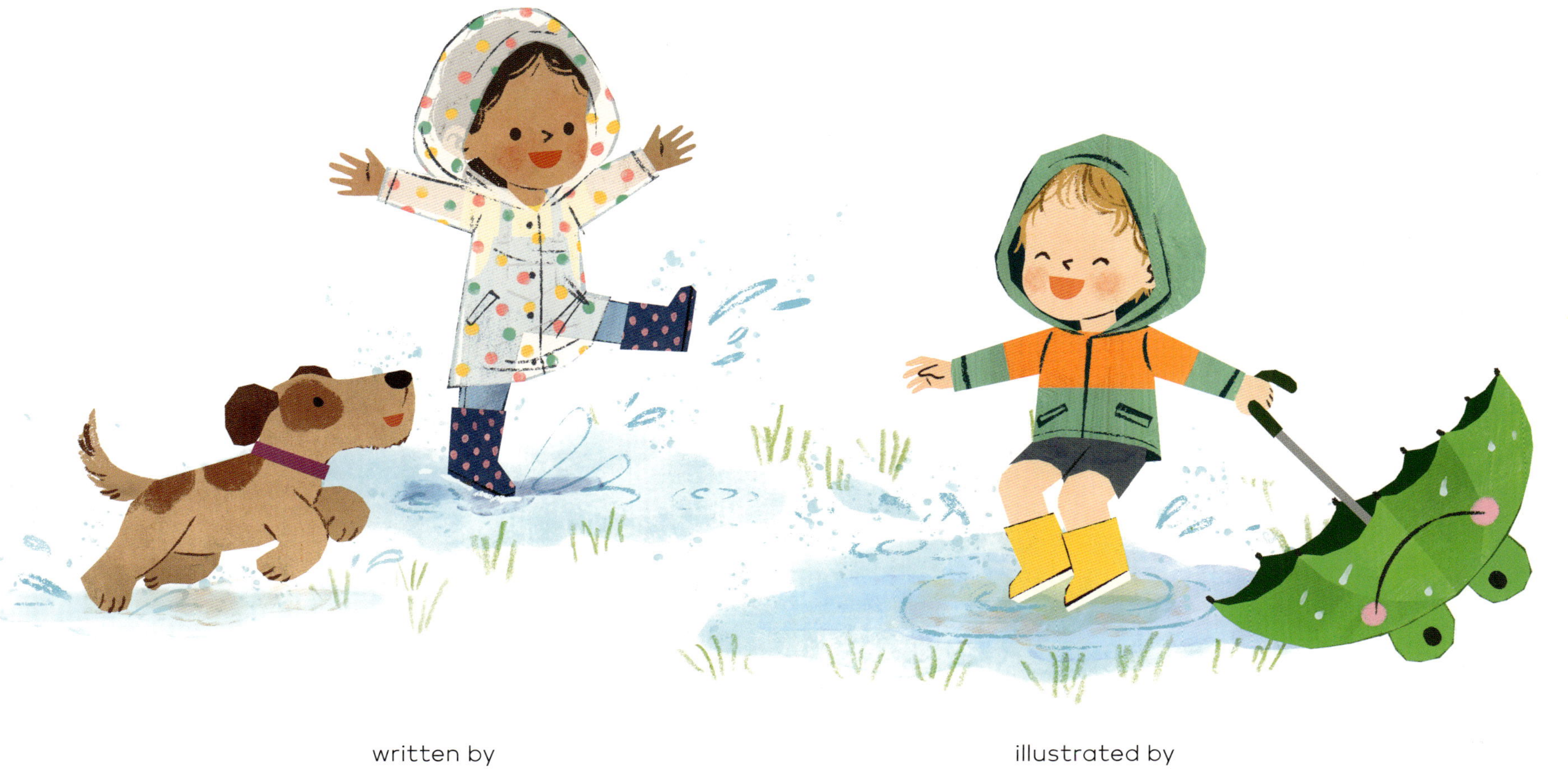

written by
Saskia Gwinn

illustrated by
Daniela Sosa

made of tiny **water drops** sparkling with dust.

They came from the sea when the sun warmed it up.

And they floated through the sky, past the birds and the planes.

The drops grew and joined together . . .

to turn into the cloud.

And when the drops were BIG . . .

And turned into **raindrops** that sped through the sky . . .

And sent **rabbits** to their burrows and **birds** to their nests...

... before tasty snacks poked their heads above the ground.

The rain helped the plants to make . . .

The sun shone on the raindrops and . . .

The rain filled the **puddles**, the **rivers** and **streams**.

It gave thirsty animals water to drink.

The rivers rolled out into . . .

...the sea.

Little by little, the cloud **disappeared**.

Then the sun warmed the water . . .

. . . and it all started again!